THE HORNS OF EVANGELINA

THE HORNS OF EVANGELINA

Published by House Of Morgue

For contact information visit:
www.houseofmorgue.com

ISBN   978-0-6151-4363-7

FIRST EDITION

10 9 8 7 6 5 4 3 2 1

This book is dedicated to my friends and family who have supported my creativity over the years. This book is the first fruit of my endless daydreaming and procrastinating pursuit of self-expression. Thank you for everything. I hope you enjoy this.

THE HORNS OF EVANGELINA

No kind of sensation is keener and more active than pain; its impressions are unmistakable.

Marquis de Sade

ONE

"Tell me something."

Joseph thinks for a second, then responds. "I love you."

"Tell me something else," she says.

Joseph tries to find some words, something to make the moment perfect, but finally offers simply "I don't know what you want me to say."

Joseph does love Allison. Really and truly he does. Just saying so should be enough. But he knows better. She expects a little more. Sure, she's over a year older than he is, and she's not the brightest girl he's ever known, but she makes him feel complete. She makes him feel safe.

He hasn't seen her in two weeks. It's almost unbearable. It never gets any easier.

When he's out on the rig, working his ass off sand blasting walls, or mixing mud, or carrying oil pipes up steep narrow stairs, he is in constant distraction. Thinking about her.

Allison Endicott.

He likes to think that she is thinking of him as well. And she is. She is always thinking about him. Even when there is still a few days before he'll be coming home, she can feel that little twinge in her crotch. And the wetness. And the tension. She misses him so much. Her fingers can only sustain her for so long.

"Just say what you want," Allison tells him.

A menacing grin creeps over Joseph's face.

"Take off your pants," he says.

"Just my pants?"

"Your panties, too."

Allison does as she is told. The smell of her desire clouds the interior of Joseph's truck almost as soon as her tender flesh is exposed.

Joseph hunkers down on the floorboard and puts his lips to her, and her eyes roll back into her head. When his tongue slips in and touches her clit, she is already cumming.

But there's no need to rush.

They are going to be here for a while.

————————

Joseph puts his shirt back on while Allison is pulling up her pants. She gets halfway and stops.

"I can hardly move," she says.

"Sorry."

Allison just smiles and gives him that look that says "Don't be sorry," without actually saying anything at all.

"We should go out tomorrow," he tells her. "Go eat someplace. I could really go for a steak."

"Sounds nice."

She leans over and kisses him, and then opens the passenger side door.

"You'll call me when you get home?"

"Yeah."

She tells him to be careful, and then turns to go into her house. Her parents wanted her in by ten. It's almost eleven. But they won't mind. They trust Joseph. Probably as much as Allison does.

Joseph watches Allison go inside, and then starts his truck. He gets his cell phone and speed dials the first saved number.

Joseph's father answers the phone.

"Hello?"

"Hey, I'm on my way home."

"Okay. Be careful."

"Do you want me to wake you when I come in."

"No. We'll see you tomorrow."

"Okay."

Joseph hangs up his cell, and pulls out of Allison's driveway.

———————

The long highway out of Monterey, Louisiana, is dark and quiet. There doesn't seem to even be any bugs in the air. Everything is dry and still.

Joseph cracks his window, allowing the thundering guitars of AC/DC, "Night Prowler" is playing in his CD player, to slip out into the night, along with smoke from his joint.

It's the middle of November, but you'd never know it here. In Louisiana, November tends to be rather warm and humid. You're lucky if you need a coat by the time Christmas rolls around.

The air conditioner in Joseph's truck is in need of repair, so the vague breeze coming in through the window is welcome. He pushes the accelerator up to 70, so the breeze gets a little more acute.

He's moving so fast that he doesn't notice the Jeep parked just off the road.

———————

Michelle is thinking to herself, "Cliff didn't spit out all of his tobacco."

Cliff does that a lot. He spits out his Skoal, but there are still little strings of tobacco in his mouth. And now, as he kisses Michelle, their tongues twirling together, it's all that Michelle can do to keep from getting sick.

"Is it time yet?" She asks.

"No," Cliff answers as he tries to kiss her again.

"It's just real spooky out here. I don't like it."

"Come on babe, I told you. We gotta meet the guy at midnight. It's barely eleven."

"Well, can we at least go somewhere else. There's not even any traffic out here."

Just then a streak of headlights flash by, and Cliff gets a glimpse at the small green truck.

"Son of a bitch," he says.

"What is it, baby?"

"You didn't see that truck?"

"What about it?"

"I think that was that Joseph Ethans boy. The boy that got my brother locked up."

Cliff sits for a few moments in silence, thinking hard to himself.

"Cliff, I don't want to do anything stupid tonight. We've got to meet that guy in a while."

"Just a little weed, babe. But this little shit's gotta get what's coming to him."

Michelle winces as Cliff's Jeep spins tires, throwing gravel, and fires out onto the highway.

"What are you gonna do?" Michelle asks.

"I'm just gonna fuck with him a little."

Cliff takes his Jeep up to 85 and barrels after the small green truck.

———————

Joseph is feeling pretty damn good now. In just a few minutes he'll be on the levee, out of Monterey. If it weren't for his girlfriend, he'd have no reason to come into this shitty little town.

It's not even a town really. Couple hundred people. The one school runs everything from kindergarten to high school. His girlfriend's graduating class had maybe 30 people in it, if that many. This town doesn't even have a mayor. But for some god awful reason, Johnny Cash felt obliged to mention this place, ever so briefly, in his song "I've Been Everywhere, Man." Of course he could have meant Monterey, California, but that was a point for argument in this back roads town.

The fishing is good. That's why most people come to Monterey. There are two lakes, interconnected, just filled with fish. Catfish. Bass. White perch. Gar. And it's the kind of place that gets joked about. Everyone in Monterey is related to one another, or the place is full of crazy backwater hicks. There are jokes about the significant lack of blacks in the town. Jokes about the fact that 30 years ago, the town didn't have electricity.

But then again, there are probably a hundred small towns in Louisiana just like this. Joseph is from Vidalia, which sits on the Mississippi River, across the bridge from Natchez, Mississippi. Vidalia is more of a traditional small town. Fast food joints. Video rental stores. A little more his speed, but still suffocating. This is why he opted to find work offshore. To spend two weeks at a time away from this place. Make enough money to go out of town and have fun when he is home. Maybe get an apartment sometime soon. Get Allison to move in. Then he'd have no reason to come to Monterey.

And that suits him just fine.

These thoughts run through his pot-tainted mind, when he suddenly notices something beside his truck. He looks out, and there is a Jeep in the opposite lane, running beside him. There are two people in the Jeep. A man is driving, and he is kinda trashy, a little heavy. A girl is in the passenger seat. Equally trashy, but kind of cute. The driver is motioning to Joseph to roll down his window. So he does.

"Hey are you Joseph Ethans?" Cliff yells out.

"Yeah..." Joseph answers.

"My brother is Bobby Dale," Cliff says.

Joseph gets a funny feeling deep down in his stomach, uncomfortable, and the expression on his face changes to fit.

"I'm gonna kick your ass, boy."

Joseph is suddenly sober as Christ on Christmas, and he stomps down hard on the accelerator, pushing his truck up over 90, over 100, almost 110.

Cliff does his best to keep up, but his Jeep is a little out of shape, and soon he is left about a quarter mile behind

Joseph's truck.

"Little fucker ain't getting away that easy."

Joseph's pulse is racing as fast as his truck, if not faster. He remembers Bobby. It was about a month ago, Joseph bought five ounces of marijuana from Bobby Dale only to get pulled over a few minutes later. Joseph struck a quick deal with the detective, and turned in Bobby, who was arrested with nearly three hundred pounds of marijuana in his mobile home, as well as a small meth lab and a considerable amount of crack cocaine. Joseph walked with a warning. He was always able to do things like that. Get in trouble, and talk his way out. Something tells him this time may be a little different.

While trying desperately to work out some kind of plan in his head, and at the speed he is currently traveling, he barely has time to register the small deer crossing the road in front of him. He throws his foot down on the brakes as the deer hits the front of his truck and comes crashing through the wind shield.

Cliff and Michelle look at each other, as the small red taillights ahead of them leave the road and vanish in the darkness.

"I think he ran off the road," Michelle says.

"Well," Cliff says, "we'll find out in a minute."

Cliff's Jeep slows down when they notice the black tire marks in the highway, which lead off to the left and into a field. A hundred feet or so from the road, they see Joseph's truck, wedged into a line of trees.

Cliff puts the Jeep in park, and he and Michelle get out. As they approach the truck, Michelle asks "Do you think he's alright?"

"If he ain't dead now," answers Cliff, "he'll wish he was when I get through with him."

The dark is quiet and still, the only sound is the hissing sound coming from the engine of Joseph's truck. Cliff and Michelle are within twenty feet of the truck when the driver's door opens and Joseph slowly staggers out. It's too dark to see him very well, but Cliff and Michelle stop and wait quietly.

Joseph walks awkwardly, sliding against the side of his truck, and comes about six feet towards Cliff and Michelle. He makes a small gurgling noise that could be either "Help me," or perhaps "Kill me," then he collapses to the ground.

"Son of a bitch," Cliff says. "I think the little fucker is dead."

He looks at Michelle. "Go check him out."

"Why the hell should I do it?"

"Because you're the goofy bitch that spent a year in nursing school and dropped out."

Michelle reluctantly nods, and takes a few steps towards Joseph, then she abruptly stops. "I can't do it, Cliff. Shit like this is why I dropped out of that school."

"Well what the hell should we do then? Just leave him here?"

Michelle is staring at Cliff, and makes not a sound. Her eyes have grown wide.

"What the hell is wrong now?" Cliff asks, realizing she's not looking at him but just past him, and he turns around just in time to be struck in the forehead with a baseball bat.

Cliff hits the ground with a thud, and Michelle tries to scream, but the muscles in her throat are frozen solid. In the darkness she watches the figure come toward her, raising the baseball bat high. She can't see his face, but as the bat comes down upon her, just before the world goes black, she thinks to herself, it must be her imagination, but it almost looks like there are antlers on his head.

TWO

It's cold and damp in the tiny room when Cliff opens his eyes. He's not sure where he is, what has happened, or if he is even awake at all. He notices an uncomfortable tension in his shoulders, and he realizes his hands are shackled to a chain above his head.

In the darkness of the room he can't see a thing. But he hears something. A voice perhaps. No, it's two voices. Two men. Not in the room, but somewhere close by.

He can't make out what the men are saying, but it sounds serious. Then one of them laughs, and Cliff gets an uneasy feeling in his stomach. He remembers now. Chasing that Ethans boy, who wrecked his truck, he remembers arguing with Michelle ("*Where the hell is she?*"), and he remembers someone coming up from behind him, clocking him a good one on the head.

"Somebody sure gonna get their ass kicked," Cliff thinks to himself. Weakness over takes him then, and he passes out, dangling from the chain.

———————

Michelle hangs from her shackles, but has failed to wake up yet. Instead she is dreaming about the love of her life. No, not Cliff. No, in her dreams, she is always with Todd Powell.

In this particular dream, Michelle is 15 again. Todd is 20. That's the way it was, and the way she wishes it could be again.

In the dream, they are at her Uncle Raymond's lake house at Lake St. John, in Ferriday, Louisiana. They are sitting out on the pier, watching the sunrise, staring at the beauty of the reflection of the sun in the dark water.

This of course never actually happened. What had really happened the one time they went up there was that her uncle caught them in the laundry room, Michelle on her knees, with Todd's dick in her throat. They were banned from the lake house after that.

But right now, in her dream, they are merely watching the sunrise.

Todd looks to Michelle and says something, low and inaudible.

"What?" Michelle asks him.

He speaks again, but she still can't hear him. He's sitting right beside her, this doesn't make any sense.

Then she hears him. "I never really loved you."

She can't believe what she's hearing. Then, as if she's not bothered enough, behind them she notices a deer standing on the bank of the lake, by the other end of the pier. "Look at that," she says. But now she doesn't want to. The deer stands up on it's back legs. It's bigger now, bulkier. Freaky looking.

"Come on and get her, I don't want her," Todd yells out to the deer-creature, which comes running down the pier. Todd just sits there as Michelle gets up in horror, backing away. She is so scared, and now she has backed up so far, she falls backwards off the pier.

When she expects to hit the water, she doesn't. Instead she just keeps falling. And crying. And moaning.

In the tiny dark room, Michelle wiggles a bit from the shackles above her head, and groans. She doesn't realize that she is not alone.

————

Joseph's head is killing him when he finally opens his eyes. Every one of his muscles feels like they've gone twelve or maybe thirty rounds with George Foreman. The pain is so intense he can hardly breathe.

He tries to look around, to get some bearing on his situation, but one of his eyes is sealed shut.

"Why do I have glue in my eye?" He ponders quietly, but then he realizes it's not glue. It's blood. Dried blood.

Now he remembers everything. Well, maybe not everything, but enough that he's not totally confused anymore.

The deer had come crashing through the windshield, kicking wildly with its legs at Joseph's face before landing in the back seat.

Then came the tree, and the loud, booming crash you only hear from inside a car accident. It's like a giant bass note pulsating through the air, and it leaves your ears ringing. Dust from the air bag floating all around, and he had tried to get out of the truck.

He remembers seeing people there, and he had tried to

walk toward them. He didn't know who they were, but he knows now.

"I am such a fucking idiot." He shakes his head in the darkness.

He feels the heavy chains above his head. He is now trying to figure out why he is shackled. Did that guy, Bobby's brother, do this to him? And why?

"Would you like some water?"

The voice startles Joseph, and he goes stiff. Trying to see through the darkness. There is a faint hint of light coming from under a door, and he can make out the figure of a girl leaning on the wall near the door.

At first, Joseph thinks it's the girl from the Jeep. But no, this girl is smaller.

"I can give you a little water, but not much."

Her voice is so soft, and curious.

Joseph tries to speak, but he is suddenly extremely

nervous. So he nods his head "yes."

The girl comes up close to him, and she holds a water bottle up to his lips, and allows some to run into his mouth. He didn't feel thirsty when she asked, he just didn't know what to do. But the water now was very welcome. He let the cool liquid calm his nerves, and soothe his throat.

"What's your name?" She asks.

"Joseph. Joseph Ethans."

"I can't tell you my name. Not right now."

Joseph's eyes are beginning to adjust more to what little light is available, and he can sort of make out the girl's face.

"You look familiar," he says. "Do I know you?"

"I doubt it. I don't get out much."

They stare at each other for a moment.

"I should probably leave now. If they catch me down here..."

The girl starts to walk away.

"Wait, you've got to help me," Joseph achingly pleads.

He sees the girl stop at the door, and look back at him. He tries to speak again, but his head begins to spin. As the girl opens the door to leave, a flood of light pours into the room, and Joseph once again succumbs to unconsciousness.

THREE

When Sheriff Deputy Collin Monroe gets the phone call at 6:00 AM to come out to Evangelina Plantation, he doesn't think much about it. Young people in Monterey are always running their vehicles off the road. He hates to think about it, but it seems like kids around here start driving when they're eight years old. They probably start drinking earlier than that.

"I might be from this place," he's admitted more than once, "but I've got no respect for the hick mentality that thrives in this little town."

Collin Monroe dropped out of technical school in the mid 80's. He had been trying to get a degree in drafting, with every intention of getting a nice job with a big architectural group and leave Monterey behind for good. Of course, things don't always turn out the way you plan.

Collin's mother had become ill. Dangerously ill. His father had died when he was a kid, so Collin quit school, came home, and enrolled in a police academy while tending to his mother's needs. Now he's with the Concordia Parish Sheriff Department, has a wife and two kids, and even took up painting several years ago. So things aren't all that bad. But then again, he's still taking care of his mother. His eternally dangerously ill mother.

One might think that life is easy and quiet in Monterey. And for the most part, that's the truth. But like any small town, there are the occasional interesting incidents.

A cheerleader is decapitated in a car accident. An old man, or a mistreated queer, commits suicide. A cop answers his front door at three in the morning, only to be shot in the face by some teen he'd been supposedly harassing.

And of course, there's this little green pickup truck, abandoned in the tree line by Cross Bayou Creek, bordering Evangelina Plantation. The truck sits, crushed into a tree, with a young deer laying dead in the small back seat.

Sheriff Deputy Collin Monroe approaches an officer standing near the truck.

"Hey Carl. What have we got?"

"Well, we found a wallet on the floor board."

He hands the wallet to Collin, who opens it and examines the license. "Joseph Ethans. Vidalia, Louisiana. Anybody call someone about this?"

"We got in touch with his folks," The other cop says. "Turns out the kid's been missing since Tuesday night."

"The truck's been here for two days?"

"Looks like it."

"And no sign of the kid?"

"Just some bloody handprints on the side of the truck."

Collin goes over to the truck to examine the blood for himself. When he spots some blood on the ground, he follows it. When the trail goes cold, he stops.

"This blood only leads out about ten feet, then it's gone."

The other cop just looks at him. "Yeah, we noticed."

"So where's the kid?"

"My guess is he's laying out here somewhere."

"Do you have a search team yet?"

"Working on it."

"Kid could be alive. We need to get moving. I'll get us some dogs out here."

The other cop nods his head, and walks off. Collin peers inside the truck to look at the bloody deer carcass.

"Fucked up shit."

A loud clacking sound draws his attention from the truck. Out in the field, only a hundred yards away, two large bucks have locked their antlers together. They are fighting, pulling against one another, trying to get free.

Collin stares for a moment. He's never seen deer fighting this close before. He gets a stale feeling deep in his gut and he turns away.

———————

"You awake, boy?"

Joseph opens his eyes to the damp darkness of the tiny room. In the faint light he can just make out the figure of a tall, thin man standing just a few feet away.

"I gotta get you ready for dinner," the Thin Man says.

"Where's the girl?" Joseph tries to ask, but his voice cracks. His mouth and throat are so dry it hurts to even speak.

"Oh don't you worry none about her. We got her locked up too. Her and your other friend."

The Thin Man pauses for a moment, and then grins.

"Of course, from the way they was talking about you, I

don't think they was your friends at all, huh?"

Joseph knows the man misunderstood him. He wasn't asking about the girl from the Jeep, he could care less about her or that Cliff guy. No, he was asking about the young girl who had come to see him. Or had he maybe dreamed that? He's not sure. And he's still too weak to argue about it.

"Hope you like deer. That's almost the only thing we eat out here."

Joseph just looks at the man. He is so hungry, but he knows that something bad is coming. He can feel it. He just can't figure out what it is.

"I'm gonna unlock your chains," the Thin Man says. "You try anything funny, and I gotta use this."

The Thin Man holds up something in the dark. Looks like a baseball bat. "And boy do I love to use it."

The Thin Man laughs to himself as he reaches up and fondles with the shackles. With a few clicks, Joseph drops down to the ground.

"Think you can walk, boy?"

Joseph doesn't make a sound. He thinks his short fall may have cracked a rib. Or maybe it's from the wreck. Doesn't matter. It hurts like hell, either way.

"Well, guess I'll have to take you there the easy way."

The Thin Man reaches down and grabs Joseph by one of his arms.

"You're gonna wish you'd stayed asleep, boy."

FOUR

"I wish I'd stayed asleep."

Sheriff Deputy Collin Monroe looks out over the vast fields of Evangelina Plantation. All you can see out here is the dirt and dead grass where corn is usually planted, the long lines of trees that surround the fields, and the tall bundle of grain elevators a few miles away.

Of course, there is also the hundred or so people, either on foot, on ATV, or on horseback, searching every foot of this area for any sign of Joseph Ethans. They've been searching for almost two days. They've searched the same places two or three times, at least. And they are just as empty handed as when they started.

Collin is beginning to agree with some of the others. Joseph Ethans might not be out here. He may have been picked up, taken somewhere. He might be alive somewhere. He might be dead, dumped in some other parish, or in the Mississippi River, just several miles away.

Collin doesn't want to think about it though. Not after meeting the boy's family. Such nice people. Not quite people he'd want to know on a social level, but good people. They love their son, and they want to see him again. They want to hear him speak.

And then there's the girlfriend. Allison Endicott. Skinny as a twig. But a cute little number. As devastating as this situation is, when he sees Allison walking around, he can't help his more perverse thoughts. Especially when he sees her crying. He'd like to comfort her, tell her things are going to be fine. Rub her back. Get her comfortable. Then try to put his hand down her pants.

No. He shouldn't think like this. This kind of thing got him in trouble several years ago. Bonnie, his wife, was ready to leave him. But he got her to stay. And he's been good since then. For the most part.

But inside his head, where no one can see, he molests every girl he sees. It's irritating at times. He knows he should probably see a shrink or something. But why bother. Might as well enjoy his imagination. It's a lot safer than the real thing. Nobody gets hurt.

"Deputy Monroe!"

Collin turns around to see a heavy set man walking towards him. "God dammit," he says under his breath.

Paul King is a reporter for the Natchez Democrat, the main newspaper for Natchez, Mississippi. Collin hates anyone from Natchez, especially the morons working at the newspaper. People in Natchez think they are living in New Orleans. But it's really just a decrepit old city, where unemployment is high, the economy is nonexistent, and the people are fools for letting it stay that way.

When he was a kid, Collin loved driving the 40 or so miles to Natchez. Go to the movies, go to the golf course, or the mall. But now, he doesn't even like going there for groceries.

The city is a joke. A big joke, with no punchline in sight.

"Care to make a statement, Collin?"

Collin just looks at Paul King, much in the way that a cat raised on corn-fed rats would look at a bowl of dry processed cat food.

"No, Paul. I'm a little busy here. Got a kid missing, you know."

"Hey, that's what I hear pal. What's the situation anyway? Foul play?"

"I don't have time for this, Paul."

Collin tries to walk away, but Paul steps out in front of him.

"Hey level with me, pal. You got a job to do, I understand that. But I got a job to do too, you know. So a little help here, would be appreciated. The sooner I do my job, the sooner I'll be out of the way."

Collin knows that fighting any harder will only make things worse. Paul's not going to leave him alone. The only way to make any progress here is to entertain the little weasel.

"Alright, Paul. You got five minutes."

"That's all I need."

Collin leads Paul several yards away, closer to the highway.

"Lay it on me," Collin says. More of a groan really.

"What kind of connection have you guys made to the other disappearances?"

"What other disappearances?"

"Well, as I'm sure you know, and you should know if you're a cop worth your badge in gold, this ain't the first time some kid has come up missing around here. Two years ago, two guys from Tennessee went missing just outside of Natchez. Their car was found abandoned just ten miles south of the city. And the year before that, some girl from Jena, Louisiana, reported her husband missing. He'd gone hunting or something, and never came home."

"I don't see what any of that has to do..."

"I know, it's been a few years, and these instances were a little out of town from here, but these occurred near heavily wooded areas. You take a look out past these fields, and you will agree with me, we are surrounded by heavily wooded areas."

"That can be said of anywhere in a thousand mile range of here, Paul. Can't you waste my time with something better than this?"

"Hey, pal, I'm just pointing out the eerie similarities. I'm saying there's a chance that kid ain't even here. He might not be in a hundred miles of here."

"That's a possibility, but for now we're concerned with searching where we can."

"Have you found anything yet?"

Collin doesn't answer. He catches himself looking down at the ground, but then looks up again.

"You been out here, what... two days? And you ain't found a damn thing, have you?"

Collin remains quiet.

"The kid might still be alive, Collin. He might be somewhere, just waiting for someone to find him. But you guys are wasting your time, searching the same fields over and over. It's time to move the search, I would think. It's what I would do if I were in charge."

"Well, you're not. I am. And as long as I am in charge here, things are gonna go as I see fit."

"Well, enjoy it while you can. I understand the kid's parents are thinking of bringing in some private investigators."

"They can do whatever they want. I can't stop them."

"I know it's getting tough out here. Hell, I still got a fucking houseful of my wife's family from New Orleans. The damn flood washes all the coon asses out of the city for the first time in forever, and they all end up in my god damn house. I got plenty of problems of my own. My boss is breathing down my neck to milk this fucking story for everything. I think she's hoping you'll find his body, mauled by a bear or something, and I can get the scoop while it's fresh. We're just a little paper, you know, but she thinks we're the god damn New York Times or something."

"Are we done, Paul?"

"Yeah... what the hell. I got enough quotes from the family. I need to get some of this shit typed up anyway. I'll be back though."

"I know."

"Good luck."

Collin's not sure if Paul is being sincere, or just being

pretentious. He thanks him anyway. When Paul is far enough away, Collin walks back out into the field. Maybe they are wasting their time. Maybe the kid's not here. Maybe they'll never find him. But there is no choice but to press on, stick to the plan. Search these fields for another day, and if there is no progress, then it's out of his hands. The state will take over. Collin will go home. This town will move on with life. Either they find the kid, or they don't. Collin gets a paycheck either way.

"Officer Monroe?"

Collin watches as Malcolm Ethans walks up to him. Collin's heart sinks a little, but he doesn't let it show.

"I saw you talking to Paul King," Malcolm says.

"Yeah. He was doing more talking than me, I guess."

"Did he tell you we're gonna call in some other detectives?"

"He mentioned it. I don't think they'll have any better luck finding your brother though."

"We're not calling them to find Joseph."

"You're not?"

"No, we want them to find whoever killed him."

"We don't know that Joseph is... we... we still have a chance of finding him."

"I'm willing to accept that my brother is dead, Officer Monroe."

"Deputy Monroe..."

"Whatever."

Malcolm has so much anger in his face, it almost intimidates Collin. Malcolm is a few years older than Joseph, but still much younger than Collin. Collin tries to imagine losing a younger brother. But he can't. Maybe if he had one.

"I promise you, Malcolm. I'll do everything I can to find your brother. And anybody who may be responsible in some way for all this."

Malcolm doesn't say anything. Collin looks around, and sees Allison leaning against her car.

"She's taking it pretty hard," Collin says, nodding towards Allison.

"Yeah."

"Do you know her?"

"Joseph brought her over a few times. I met her once. I'm not at home much."

"Go talk to her. She could use some reassurance. You got your whole family keeping each other going. She doesn't have anybody right now."

"Yeah..."

Malcolm walks off, towards Allison. Collin looks around, realizing he is alone again, at last. He takes a deep breath, enjoys a quiet moment, then heads back out into the field.

FIVE

When Joseph wakes up, he is being dragged by his arms up a steep set of old, splintery stairs. It's dark, but he can see some light shining down from above.

When they reach the top of the stairs, Joseph is dragged even further, across a wood floor, down a long hallway, and into a large well-lit room.

There is a huge table, with chairs, in the middle of the room.

"Hope you're feeling hungry, boy," the Thin Man says, as he pulls Joseph up and sits him into one of the old chairs.

It is now that Joseph realizes there are other people sitting at the table. A man and a woman, tied into their seats, with hoods covering their heads.

The Thin Man ties Joseph into his chair, and Joseph gives no resistance. He's too weak to fight back, and still isn't entirely sure he's not having some fucked up dream.

"Critter, what the fuck are you doing?"

Joseph looks over towards the sound of the voice. He sees another thin man, dressed in camouflage. He seems a little cleaner than the guy who dragged him here, Critter apparently.

"Why the fuck ain't he wearing a hood?"

Critter looks puzzled for a moment. "I didn't think about it, Teddy. The kid was all passed out and shit."

"Well, you know James ain't gon' like this at all. You better hope that kid ain't getting a good look at this place."

"I'm sorry, Teddy. Gimme a fuckin break, man. The

kid's practically asleep right now."

Teddy stares at Joseph. Joseph tries looking back, but the light still hurts his eyes, and his vision is a little fuzzy.

"Just put a goddamn hood on him now, before James gets in here."

Critter walks over to grab a hood from out of a cardboard box. "Dinner ready yet?"

"Ten minutes," Teddy says, leaving the room.

"Hear that boy? Won't be long. Gonna have us a nice little meal, soon."

Everything goes black, as Critter pulls the hood down over Joseph's head.

"Try not to get into anything," Critter says, laughing.

All Joseph can see is darkness. He hears some shuffling, then he hears Critter walking away, and shutting a door behind him.

Now everything is silent.

Joseph wants to pass out again, but he has this terrible feeling he's not going to be sleeping again anytime soon.

He thinks about Allison. Wondering what she's doing. Is she worried about him yet? Does anyone know he's missing? He doesn't even have any idea how long it's been since the wreck.

"Is that you, Joseph?"

An unmistakable voice. It's Bobby Dale's brother. The one who was driving the jeep. Joseph feels himself getting very nervous now.

"Yeah..." Joseph answers.

"Where the fuck are we at?"

"What do you mean?"

"I mean, where the fuck are we at?"

Joseph doesn't understand. "How the hell should I know?"

"One of those guys said you weren't wearing no hood

when they brought you in."

It's now that Joseph realizes that Cliff is the man at the table. Wearing a hood.

"You ain't got nothing to do with this?" Joseph asks.

Cliff is getting irritated now. "Fuck no, you little shit! Now, do you know where we are or not?"

Joseph thinks for a moment, trying to remember something about the place. But he apparently hadn't been paying much attention when they were dragging him around.

"No. The place was too dark to see anything."

"Shit."

Michelle starts crying deep under her own hood.

"Come on baby, don't start that shit now. I'm gonna get us out of this."

"How the hell do you plan to do that. We can't even see where the hell we are."

"We just gotta stay calm, baby. We keep our heads straight, maybe we can work something out."

"Cliff... one of them fucked me."

Cliff goes silent. The whole room is silent, except for Michelle's sobbing.

"What do you mean 'fucked you?'"

"I mean they fucking raped me, goddamnit!"

Cliff is silent for a few more moments. "Those mother fuckers. I get one goddamn chance I'm gonna fuck up the first mother fucker I can reach."

Cliff is about to rant some more, but he is interrupted by a faint laughter nearby.

The faint laughter spreads to several more, and within seconds, the entire room is filled with laughter.

The hoods are pulled from all three captives, and they are shocked to find the table surrounded by people. All of them rough looking. The only one of them not laughing is

Teddy, who after a moment finally speaks up.

"All right, shut it up. Boss is coming."

The laughter dies down, and the men all get vaguely serious. They pull their chairs back from the table, but do not sit down.

All heads turn to the far end of the room, where a door opens. In walks a heavy set man with dark hair, and a thick dark mustache.

He steps up to the head of the table, pulls his chair back and sits down. The other men sit down as well.

Everyone is quiet, as the man looks over the three captives. He finally sets his eyes on Joseph.

"What's your name, son?"

Joseph is scared to death. Almost too scared to speak. But somehow he manages to force his vocal chords.

"Joseph. Joseph Ethans."

"Well, Joseph Ethans. My name's James. James

Hennessy. This is my house. You are my guest."

Cliff interrupts, "Guest? What the fuck kind of people treat a guest like this?"

James reaches out and smacks Cliff hard across the face.

Cliff explodes with rage. "You mother fucker, why don't you untie me and try that again!"

James, ignoring Cliff's outcry, gets out of his chair, walks over to Joseph, and smacks him as well. Joseph just stares up at him.

"I kinda like this one," James says. "He's a little small. But the big guy's got too much temper. He'd be a good, hard worker, but I dunno."

He looks them both over. "It's gonna be a tough call."

"What about the bitch?" Critter pipes in.

James walks over to Michelle. He reaches out, gently caressing her face with his hand. Tears are streaming down her cheeks.

"She's just a little crybaby. We ain't got no need for her anyway."

Everyone gets anxious expressions on their faces.

"Can we take her to the pit?" Critter asks.

"That's not a bad idea," James responds.

"What about dinner?" Teddy asks.

"Dinner can wait!" Another man calls out. The room fills with hoots and hollers. James finally gestures to them to calm down.

"Okay. Okay... The pit it is."

Everyone yells out with excitement once more. James looks at Cliff and Joseph. "You boys ain't gonna want to miss this."

SIX

The feeling of dread grows colder with every step they take. Or every foot they are dragged. Joseph, Cliff and Michelle are being moved down a long corridor. Their captors didn't even bother with the hoods this time.

The air is stale, and the walls are made of stone. Joseph is reminded of an old horror movie, something from the 60s. Some vampire movie, with a haunted castle and underground catacombs.

He knows whatever is at the end of this corridor will not be very pleasant.

Michelle is being dragged, sobbing and moaning, at the front of the line by Teddy. Cliff would love nothing more than to pound each one of these guys' skulls in. He finds himself watching closely, waiting for that perfect moment to make his move. But he knows he's being watched. And there are so many of these freaks around him.

The fourteen or so men from the dining room, plus the ones known as Critter and Teddy. And then the boss, James Hennessy, walks in the rear of the procession.

Suddenly the line of people comes to a halt. Before them is a huge wooden door. James goes to the door, pulls out a set of keys and unlocks the ancient looking door. As the door swings open, Joseph half expects to see old torture devices or some strange temple room. He is a little surprised and disturbed when he sees only a large open room, with a hole dug in the center.

The pit is about thirty feet in diameter, and just about as deep. There is a smell of rot and sweat in the room; smells of piss and shit. And this heavy feeling of discomfort in the air around them.

Even the madmen who have brought them here, even

they seem a little uneasy going into the room. All that changes when they hear the grunting.

"Tie them to the posts," James says, and Cliff and Joseph are lead to the edge of the pit and tied up to two of the large wooden posts that encircle the pit.

Joseph looks down into the pit, but there is only darkness to be seen, and the terrible grunting sound from deep in that darkness.

James approaches the edge of the pit. "You boys know what LSD is? Lysergic Acid Diethylamide. Hippies and queers used to get off on the shit. Hardcore hallucinogenic drug. Only takes a little bit to get a man tripping, get him seeing things ain't really there. Well, them grunts you're hearing down there, that's a deer. A buck. A twelve point. A great big son of a bitch too. We've had him here for a couple of years now. He's kinda like a pet of ours, but he's more than that. Bring the girl over here!"

Teddy brings Michelle over to the pit.

"Start strippin' her down. Leave on her skivvies."

Teddy begins to strip away Michelle's outer layer of clothing.

"Don't you touch her, mother fucker," Cliff chimes in, but James cut him off with a punch to the gut.

"Ain't got no time for loud talkers, boy. Now back to what I was saying. We got a big ass deer down there. Feed him real good. Treat him like family. Only thing is, every once in a while, we like to have a little fun. Put a little something extra in his dinner bowl. A little bit of that LSD. Actually, we overdo it sometimes, and that buck can turn right mean."

James motions for one of the other men to come over.

"Gimme the acid."

The man hands James a small tin box.

"You're gonna give the deer acid?" Joseph asks.

"Hell no, son," James says. "We already gave him

plenty. This is for the girl."

Michelle, who is now standing frightened in only her panties and bra, is held while her mouth is forced open.

"Just a little bit, sweetheart." James pours a liberal amount of the powdered LSD into Michelle's gaping, crying mouth. Cliff begins yelling again, but he is ignored. The damage is done.

"Now, she's gonna start tripping out any second now. And since none of you boys from around here probably ain't got no experience with a drug like this, except maybe them weak-ass mushrooms from the cow pasture, something tells me this little darling is gonna be in for a pretty strong freak out."

Joseph and Cliff watch as Michelle begins crying harder, twitching and sweating.

"But that ain't the worst of it." James suddenly pushes Michelle over the edge of the pit. She screams and disappears down in the darkness.

She lands with a thud on the floor of the pit. Cliff is going ape-shit. Joseph is just staring into the darkness with terrible anticipation.

"Now we got that poor girl down there alone with that big ol' deer. Both of them are all jacked up on LSD, and probably scared of each other too."

Everyone stares down into the pit, listening to the sobs and grunts. James motions to a man standing near an electric breaker box.

"Let's get some light down there, whaddaya say!"

The man flips a series of switches, and an array of large photo flood lamps spark to life, illuminating the massive pit.

Michelle and the deer are equally startled by the sudden brightness. The deer stumbles a little, almost tripping over bones and meat that lay scattered upon the floor of the pit. The deer straightens itself, and then notices Michelle.

Michelle cries out, manages to pull herself onto her feet, and backs up defensively against the blood-caked, dirty wall.

Cliff calls out to Michelle, telling her to stay calm.

Joseph is speechless. He just stares down at the deer. The beast is enormous. He doesn't think he's ever even seen a photo of a deer this big. And it's antlers. They are just as impressive. Although something about them does not look right.

Then he realizes what it is. The antlers have been filed down to sharp points. Like a tangle of freakish spears.

The deer charges at Michelle, who scuffles out of the way, trying not to slip on the malicious goo that coats the floor of the pit. The deer charges again, and once again misses it's target.

Joseph watches this go on for a few moments. It all seems so surreal.

Michelle then reaches down and picks up a rather large bone. It looks like the thigh bone of a horse. Michelle screams madly at the deer. Joseph doesn't really catch what is said, because the entire time the room is flooded with laughter and yells from the people who have surrounded the pit, insane with glee over the mad spectacle.

The deer approaches Michelle slowly, with it's head low. It looks like it could be bowing in respect. Perhaps Michelle's weapon has scared the deer into submission.

Then the deer rears up suddenly, kicking with it's monstrous legs at Michelle, who drops the bone, and collapses to the ground.

The cheering in the room gets louder still. Cliff cries out in mercy for his girl.

The deer's mighty hooves kick and cut at Michelle's trembling flesh. Michelle screams, trying her best to fight the huge animal off of her.

Then the deer throws it's head back and thrusts it back down again, it's antlers piercing the soft flesh of Michelle's stomach. Michelle grabs the antlers in an apparent attempt to break the deer's neck, or just pull it away, but the deer jerks back suddenly, tossing Michelle's insides all over the pit.

Michelle's face tenses up in terror for a slight moment, then her entire body goes limp. The crowd cheers even louder.

The deer thrusts down again and smashes Michelle's rib cage open, spilling out more of her vital organs.

Cliff vomits all over himself, then passes out. Joseph just watches at the deer continues to stab and slice at Michelle's body, turning it into a bloody, pulpy mess.

Critter takes this opportunity to yell out "All hail the mighty Cernunnos!"

The entire room takes up the cry. "All hail the mighty Cernunnos!"

It becomes a harsh chorus. "All hail the mighty Cernunnos! All hail the mighty Cernunnos!"

Joseph manages to take his eyes off of the hellish scene below him, and he looks over to find James Hennessy staring at him.

James is the only one not chanting. Not celebrating. He looks deathly serious. He is even more menacing than the monstrous deer grinding Michelle into oblivion deep in the pit.

James stares at Joseph for a moment, then interrupts the chanting.

"All right now. Shut the fuck up! That's enough for now. It's time to get down to business."

The crowd calms down, giving their leader their undivided attention.

"Okay. Get these guys to the cutting room. I'm going to go wake my daughter. We don't have a whole lot of time to waste, so we need to get all our preparations in order."

The men pull hoods down over Cliff's and Joseph's heads. They cut them down from the poles, and drag them out of the room, back down that long corridor.

Joseph begins to let his thoughts drift. He thinks about

his family. His mother and father. He thinks about his brother.

And he thinks about Allison.

"Will I ever see you again?" He says in his head. "Will I ever see anyone I love again?"

In his mind, he begins to think harder now. Perhaps not all is lost. Perhaps there is a way out of this.

Because of the hood, he can't see anything. But he can hear pretty well, so he begins to listen. To everything. Every little sound which could help him figure out where he is, or how to get out.

He tries hard to memorize how long he is dragged, how many turns his captors make. He's sure that if he just pays a little attention, he'll figure something out.

He swears to himself, he'll get out of here. He'll get away from these psycho fucks.

He will see his Allison again. And he will see this place burn.

SEVEN

As Malcolm approaches Allison, he can't help but remember the first time he saw her. Actually, it was the second time.

He met her once, when Joseph brought her over to meet their parents, and Malcolm was introduced briefly. Malcolm had to go out, so he was a little rushed, and was not overly impressed with his brother's new girlfriend. She just looked like another skinny blonde hick.

But there was this other time. Malcolm had come home late. His parents were out of town, and when he walked in to the empty house, he didn't think much about it. But when he heard the talking coming from the bathroom, he had to check it out.

"Joe, is that you?"

There was a shuffling inside the bathroom. He heard two voices. Joseph, and a girl.

"Yeah," Joseph called out. "I'll be out in a bit."

Malcolm walked off, content to leave them alone. But a thought had occurred to him. He grabbed a pack of cigarettes, and slipped back out the front door.

Outside, he lit a cigarette, and took a few long drags. He then walked around the side of the house. The darkness of the back yard was split in two by the glowing light coming from the bathroom window. Malcolm had used this trick before, when unknown cousins from way out of town came to visit. They'd go to the bathroom, strip down for their shower, and sometimes pleasure themselves, never knowing they were being watched.

The bathroom window has no shade, just a thin lacy curtain. Anyone could walk right up and look inside. And that's just what Malcolm did.

Through the window, all he saw at first was Joseph, naked, leaning against the counter. Then he saw the girl, Allison, the skinny blonde hick, on her knees, her heading moving up and down around Joseph's crotch.

Malcolm watched as Allison stood up, and Joseph moved so she could sit on the counter. Joseph got down low, and began to eat her pussy.

Malcolm had hit the jackpot. He unzipped his pants, and began to jerk off, watching Allison as she bit her lip and rolled her eyes.

After a few minutes, Joseph sat down on the toilet, and Allison got down and straddled him. She moved up and down, grinding on Joseph's cock, and she was moaning. At this time, Malcolm and Allison were barely 3 feet from one another. If there had been no window, they'd have been staring at each other in the face.

Malcolm came, ejaculating into the grass, but he could not stop looking. He just stared at Allison. He couldn't take his eyes off of her.

Then she looked at him. Right at him. Through the window, into his eyes. Malcolm was terrified. It was impossible. *It's too dark outside for her to see me.* He had tested this out a dozen times at least. But it really seemed like she was looking at him.

Allison closed her eyes, and made a high pitched moan, and Malcolm knew that she had finished.

"Hey," Allison says, leaning against her car as Malcolm walks up from the field.

"Hey. How you holding up?"

"I've been better," Allison says. Her eyes look like those of a lost child: Tired, confused and lonely.

Malcolm walks up beside her, and leans against the car.

"I'm sorry about all this," Malcolm says.

"Why? This isn't your fault."

"I know, but somebody should say it. Joseph's whole

family is out here, and I haven't seen anybody say anything to you."

"Well, they are a little preoccupied."

"Yeah..."

"Why aren't you looking?" Allison asks.

"Because it's not doing any good."

"Yeah..."

"I don't think he's out here."

"Do you think he'll turn up?"

"I don't know."

There is a long awkward silence between the two. They both just look out in the field, as dozens of people are walking around, calling out to Joseph, and getting no response.

"Do you think he's dead?" Allison finally asks.

"I don't know... Maybe."

"Oh..."

There is silence again, but Malcolm cuts it short.

"I'm sorry. There's always a chance, you know."

"Yeah."

"This is really hurting you, huh?"

"Yeah... What about you?"

"I'm just mad, you know. I think somebody hurt my brother, bad. And they might get away with it."

Silence again. They don't know it, but they are both completely numb at this moment.

In the fields, Deputy Monroe calls over one of the other officers.

"We need to wrap this up," he says.

The other officer nods, and heads towards a group of searchers, to begin spreading the word. Tomorrow the feds will be here, and this will all be out of local hands.

"I wonder what's going on," Malcolm says, seeing the commotion building in the fields.

"I don't know," Allison says. "Do you want to get out of here?"

Malcolm looks at Allison, and says "Sure."

They get down, get into Allison's car, and drive off down the road.

Malcolm is just glad to get away from those endless fields. Allison is just glad to have someone giving her some attention.

EIGHT

Once again Joseph wakes up to that pain in his shoulders and hands. He looks up at the chains above his head, and the shackles that grip his wrists.

Once again Joseph feels that vague disconnectedness, as if he were dreaming. But he's not dreaming. He knows better.

He is in Hell.

He is somewhat surprised when he notices that Cliff is with him, likewise suspended by chains. They are alone in a large cold room. It is quiet. As far as Joseph can tell, there is nobody within talking distance of the room.

The room is vast. Tiles cover the floor and walls, with long tables boxing off the room. There are heavy chains with hooks, and a cold, raw meaty smell in the air.

"We're in a cooler," Cliff finally says, breaking the silence, but not looking up. "A cooler, and a butcher shop, I think."

Joseph looks around, and sure enough he can see large knives and meat cleavers laying on the long tables.

"Why are we in a cooler?" Joseph asks.

"I don't know," Cliff answers. "And I don't want to think about it."

Joseph's eyes are drawn to the large steel door several yards away. "We need to get out here."

"We can't."

"We HAVE to, or things are about to get really bad."

Cliff looks up at Joseph. "How can they get worse? Did you see what they did to Michelle? These people are fucking monsters. How can someone do that?"

Joseph fidgets in his shackles. "I think I can get out of these. They're not as tight as the others."

Joseph strains and grits his teeth, turning his wrists slightly, back and forth, all the while pulling down with his arms. The rusty metal cuts into the knuckles of his thumbs, and blood runs hot down his arms. The pain is intense, but the blood seems to lubricate his efforts. After a few more twists and pulls, his hands finally slip free, and Joseph falls to the cold floor below.

"Son of a bitch," Cliff says, slightly impressed.

Joseph walks over to the large steel door and presses his ear against it. He hears nothing.

Cautiously he reaches for the handle.

The door of the cooler creaks open, and Joseph sticks his head out into a long hallway. It is empty and quiet.

Cliff watches Joseph step back inside and walk over to one of the long cutting tables. Joseph grabs a knife and walks up to Cliff.

"How tight are your shackles?"

"Not too bad."

Joseph reaches up and cuts Cliff's hands, just above the shackles.

"Goddamnit! What the fuck!"

"Keep your voice down," Joseph says. "The blood will help you slip out."

It takes a few moments longer, but Cliff manages to get out of the shackles. He looks at his bleeding hands as Joseph hands him a heavy meat cleaver.

"We have to go now," Joseph says. "We're probably going to need these."

"Do you really think this will work?"

"I don't know. But if we don't try..." Joseph's words trail off as he looks around at the meat hooks and cutting tables. Images of Michelle's guts clinging to that monstrous deer's antlers flash through his mind.

"Okay," Cliff says, pulling Joseph back into the moment.

"Let's do this."

The silence of the hall is interrupted by the cooler's creaking door as Joseph and Cliff step out armed with knives and meat cleavers.

"Which way should we go?" Cliff asks.

"I don't know."

They look down both directions of the hall, which extends several hundred feet either way.

"I think we should go left," Cliff says.

"Fine with me."

The hallway is dark and stale. There are no other doors lining the walls, but there is a sharp right turn at the end. The turn leads further down to a solitary wooden door at the end.

Joseph and Cliff slowly approach the door, and Joseph puts his ear against it. "I don't hear anything."

"Should we go through?" Cliff asks.

Joseph thinks for a moment, then listens again. He hears a faint rumbling sound. Like a small engine.

"I think I hear a generator."

"Let's go in," Cliff says. Joseph can tell that Cliff is getting more anxious to get away. Joseph nods and reaches for the door knob. He starts to turn it, but he hesitates.

"What's wrong?" Cliff asks.

"I don't know. Something don't feel right."

Cliff gets a hard grimace on his face. "Goddamnit we ain't got time for this shit, let's just get the fuck out of here!"

Cliff pushes Joseph aside and opens the door wide. As they step through they are faced with the grim realization of what the small engine noise was.

Inside the room is a long table. Upon the table lays Michelle's grotesque remains. Standing over her is a tall bulky man with a leather apron, and a long beard. Joseph has just enough time to think about his resemblance to one of those guys in ZZ Top, then he sees the bloody chain saw in the man's hands.

The man had been cutting up Michelle's body, but the opening of the door had startled him, and he had spun around, throwing bloody bits of Michelle's bones and meat all over Joseph and Cliff.

Cliff freezes up at the sight of Michelle, and the bearded man is obviously surprised to see the two prisoners standing free in the room with him. Joseph seizes the moment, running the several feet toward the man, slamming a meat cleaver deep into his forehead.

The man's chain saw hits the floor, making a loud god awful noise. Another door opens up, and two men step into the room.

They see Cliff and Joseph, and they pull pistols out from under their shirts.

"Goddamnit!" Joseph yells, turning and running out of

the room, back down the long hallway. Cliff quickly follows, trying to shake the image of Michelle from his mind.

Joseph and Cliff round the corner, the two men not far behind. As they approach the cooler, two more men step out from around the corner at the other end of the hall. Joseph has little time to think, so he grabs Cliff and they rush back into the cooler.

Joseph slams the door shut, and locks it from the inside.

"What the fuck are we doing?" Cliff asks. "We can't just stay in here."

"Would you rather be out there with them?" Joseph retorts.

Joseph turns around, pushing his back against the door and lets out a sigh. Then across the room his eyes meet those of someone else in the cooler.

"Oh fuck me," Joseph says.

Cliff turns around, and sees Critter grinning at them,

holding a rifle.

"Hope you boys enjoyed your little outing," Critter says, barely holding back laughter.

"You son of a bitch!" Cliff yells out, charging out towards the thin man with both knife and cleaver raised high.

Critter calmly raises his rifle up, firing out a single shot. Cliff is hit in the leg, and he tumbles over, hitting the floor.

Critter then aims the rifle at Joseph.

"Now unlock the door, boy."

Joseph reaches back and unlocks the cooler door. The door swings open and the room fills with angry men. They grab Joseph and restrain him, while they pick Cliff up off the floor. Cliff moans in pain, as fresh blood runs from the wound in his thigh.

"Okay now," Critter says, "I think it's time we had us some real fun."

"No," a voice from the door booms out. Everyone turns to face James Hennessy, who has just walked in. "Fun time is over. Now we get down to business."

James walks up to Joseph. "Is this the one that buried the hatchet in Jim's head?"

"Yeah boss," an anonymous voice answers.

James closes his eyes, shakes his head in disapproval, and punches Joseph hard in the stomach. Joseph doubles over, trying desperately to regain his breath.

"Go fetch my daughter," James says. "We need to do this now."

One of the men does as told, and James walks over to Cliff. "Your leg hurt, son?"

"Fuck you," Cliff hisses.

James just smiles at him. "I gotta admit, I'm impressed with you boys getting out of this cooler. But you shoulda known you couldn't get far."

James looks his prisoners over for a minute. "Get their shirts off."

Joseph and Cliff give little resistance as their shirts are pulled off. The cold air of the cooler becomes a little more intense, and Joseph can feel his heart beating faster.

After a few minutes, all eyes turn towards the door again.

And there she stands.

"Rosalyn," James says to her. "Come in, darling."

The girl walks in, beautiful as anything could be. She's not quite seventeen, with still a little baby fat clinging to her body. A perfect little angel, with long beautiful red hair, walking into this freezing little Hell.

Rosalyn walks up to her father and stands beside him.

"This here is my daughter Rosalyn."

Joseph and Cliff stare at her, speechless. Her presence seems surreal.

"Darling, I hate to rush you like this, but these two boys are pretty much all we got to offer. We ain't got time to go find any more, so I'm going to need you to pick which one you can work with."

Rosalyn walks up to Joseph first, and runs her hand over his bare chest. Joseph looks into her eyes. Without saying anything, he realizes she is the girl who visited him before. She had brought him water. Treated him gently. He was now more confused than ever.

"This one is cute," she says with a playful grin, before turning and walking up to Cliff. "This one looks tough. He'd be a good worker."

"He's a little stubborn," James adds.

"Yes," Rosalyn says. "And I don't care much for his tattoo."

All eyes turn to Cliff's right upper arm, where sits a flaming skull, mouth gaping wide with rage.

"My daughter don't care much for tattoos," James says.

Rosalyn then looks back at Joseph. She eyes him for a few moments, then closes her eyes. "I want him."

James smiles. He feels his daughter has made a good choice, considering her options.

"Please escort my daughter back to her room, while we finish off things down here."

Rosalyn is walked out of the room, and the cooler door is shut.

"Put him back in the shackles," James says, motioning towards Joseph. "And make sure they're tight this time."

The men do as told, and Joseph soon finds himself dangling from shackles and chains once again.

"What about the big one?" Critter asks.

"You know," James says. "Put him on a hook."

Critter gets a wide smile on his face. Cliff asks what the fuck is going on as two of the bigger men lift him up in a single motion, and allow his body to come to rest on a large meat hook pierced through his back.

Cliff howls in pain and horror. He reaches behind his back, trying to grab the hook, trying to find a way to escape it's cold grasp. He kicks and screams wildly.

James takes a long knife from one of the cutting tables and approaches Cliff.

"Ain't nothing personal, son."

James reaches up, and makes one long cut from Cliff's throat all the way down to his groin. Cliff's eyes grow wide and bulge, as the cut separates, opening up slowly, and all the things that make Cliff tick on the inside come spilling out and down to the floor.

Joseph watches as Cliff's body goes limp, his eyes still wide, but no longer full of pain. They are just still. Turning cold in this miserable cooler.

James walks up to Joseph now, and puts the knife up to his throat. "I want you to watch this now. I want you to know this was almost you."

Joseph is too afraid to close his eyes, and sees every detail of what occurs next.

Cliff's body is lowered a little, just enough that his dead feet barely touch the floor. Cliff's shoes, pants, and underwear are removed. One of the men goes behind Cliff, and pulling his own leg up, allows his knee to rest on Cliff's tailbone. He grips Cliff's legs, and begins to pull them apart wide. The man grunts loud as he pulls back even harder, and there is a loud crunch and snap as Cliff's pelvic bones shatter and the flesh around his groin tears apart.

Next, Cliff is skinned. His thick fatty skin pulled skillfully away from his muscle and bone. Then he is quartered. His arms and legs are thrown to rest upon a nearby cutting table.

This all takes about fifteen minutes and Cliff's body is reduced to a slab of meat dangling from a hook. Only his head remains untouched, making the sight all the more surreal.

When all is done, and the remains are hosed down, allowing the blood to run to a drain in the center of the floor, James takes the knife away from Joseph's throat.

"Leave him in here for the night. Give him some time alone with his friend."

Soon, everyone leaves. And Joseph is alone. Hanging from chains in a large cooler. Trying not to look at the horror of Cliff's remains hanging just twenty feet away.

He can't fight it now. He feels hopeless. Forsaken.

He tries to say a small prayer, but instead he cries.

He cries until his eyes are numb and his throat is raw. And then he sleeps. Hoping to god that he'll have no dreams. Nothing to give him false peace from this nightmare he has stumbled into.

NINE

When Malcolm and Allison arrive at the little house, they find they are alone.

"My mom works during the day," Allison says. "And my dad is spending the week at his hunting camp."

Malcolm makes no response. He is feeling a little uncomfortable. And a little excited.

"So..." Allison starts, but gives a brief pause. "Would you like to see my room."

"Yes," Malcolm says, with no hesitation. "Yes, I would."

Allison's room is a tiny space in the rear of the house. Her walls are covered in posters of cutie-boy pop stars and kittens.

"My room has been pretty much unchanged since I was like 13," she says. "I'm not this immature or anything."

Malcolm interrupts her by grabbing her by the arms and kissing her deep. Their tongues roll over and over, and Allison moans gently.

After a minute, Allison pulls away.

"I love Joseph," she says.

"I know you do."

"This just doesn't feel right."

Malcolm is quiet for just a moment, then says "Yes it does."

They embrace each other again.

Allison slips her shirt off over her head. The last few days have hurt so much. She just wants to be held. To be kissed. To be loved. To be touched in a most intimate way. She needs this.

Her pants fall to the floor, followed by his. Then her bra. His shirt. Her panties. His boxers. They collapse upon the bed.

Malcolm lays on top of her tiny body. He stares into her beautiful eyes.

"Are you sure you want to do this?" He asks.

"Of course not," she tells him, then she reaches down and squeezes his cock. She thinks to herself "Joseph's is bigger," then she guides him into her.

She is so wet, there is no resistance. He moves in her like a machine. All that she can do is close her eyes, bite her lip, and let herself go.

Forty minutes pass, and neither have let up. By now, they are like two sweaty pigs, wrestling over the last bit of scraps. Allison has her legs wrapped around Malcolm. Malcolm has his face buried between her shoulder and neck, sucking at her neck, biting every so often.

After a few more minutes, Malcolm realizes that Allison

is crying. So he stops.

"What's wrong? Did I hurt you?"

"No. It's not that?"

"Well, what is it?"

Allison looks away, and Malcolm follows her eyes across the room to her makeup bench. Sitting on top is a large picture of Allison in a bikini. Also in the picture, holding her from behind, is Joseph.

"Oh Christ," Malcolm says. He gets up, and starts to get dressed.

"You don't have to stop," Allison tells him.

"Yes I do. I shouldn't be here. I like you. I really do. But my baby brother is still out there somewhere. I need to be out there looking."

Allison pulls a sheet over herself. "Will you come back?"

"I don't know. I just can't deal with this right now, you know?"

Allison nods, reluctantly.

"I'm sorry," she tells him. "This was my idea."

Malcolm looks at her. He wants nothing more than to get back into that bed with her, and hold her, and just sleep.

But instead, he walks out of the room. And out of the house.

Allison just lays in the bed. She feels ashamed. A little betrayed.

She looks at the picture of her and Joseph.

"I hope you're happy, you bastard."

The picture makes no response. Allison finally loses it, and cries madly into her pillow.

TEN

In the middle of the night, Joseph is awakened by the sound of someone singing in whisper.

He opens his eyes, which burn in the bright florescent light of the meat cooler, and he sees the girl, Rosalyn, sitting on an overturned crate several feet away.

She is singing softly, staring at the floor, and almost instantly she feels Joseph's gaze, and looks up to him.

"I'm sorry," Rosalyn says. "I was trying not to wake you."

"It's okay," Joseph says.

They are silent for several moments, until Joseph speaks up. "What are you doing here?"

"I wanted to see you."

"Why?" Joseph asks.

"I think you deserve an explanation."

Joseph stares at her. Seeing her fully in the light like this, he can see her beauty and perfection for the first time. He's never seen anything so beautiful in his entire life.

"What I deserve," Joseph says, "is to be let go."

"I can't do that."

"Why not?"

"Because they would kill me," Rosalyn says.

She looks away from him. It would seem she's contemplating leaving.

"They are going to kill me," Joseph finally says.

"No," Rosalyn says. "You don't need to die. As long as you follow the rules."

"I don't know what you are talking about."

"That's why I am here," Rosalyn says. "To explain to you what is going on. Now... do you want to know or should I leave?"

Joseph thinks for a few minutes. He finds her company strangely comforting, which shames him a little when he remembers Allison.

"If I listen, I can live?" Joseph asks.

"Yes," Rosalyn answers.

"Then tell me."

Rosalyn gets up from the crate, and goes to the door of the cooler. She looks out into the long hall, and satisfied no one is around, she walks back over to Joseph.

"Okay," she says. "What I am going to tell you will sound crazy, but you have to let me finish. I am putting myself at risk coming here, and I need to tell you the truth.

"My father is James Hennessy. My mother was Brighid. They met in the early 70s in Toronto, Canada, where my father was a European History teacher. My mother was from an old Irish family, with pagan religious beliefs. Do you know what a pagan is?"

"No," Joseph says.

"A pagan is basically someone who worships gods and goddesses that existed before Christianity. Romans were pagans. Native Americans were pagan. Witches are usually pagan."

"Your mother was a witch?"

"No," Rosalyn says. "Not exactly. She just loved nature and animals, and all the ancient rituals passed down through her family. Anyway, my father became interested in pagan studies, since it tied in with a lot of the research he'd done into European history. He eventually combined the two, and began working on a book that would delve into the pagan history of Europe, in particular the old Celtic regions in Britain and Ireland, as well as Italy."

"I don't understand what this has to do with me,"

Joseph says.

"I'm trying to get to that," Rosalyn says, irritated by the interruption. "When my parents got married, they went to explore Europe, to see old pagan architecture and artifacts, to study the old gods and goddesses and how the old beliefs where buried under oppression from the rising powers of Rome and the Christian church. My mother and father fell in love with a god known as Cernunnos, the god of nature, the god of the wild.

"Little was known about this god. He was found in art and writings all over Europe, and he was represented by the image of a man with antlers growing from his head. He was known as The Horned God. He was worshipped by hunters and farmers, as well as looked upon as a symbol of strength and sexuality, and power and wealth. Cernunnos is found in many religions under different names. In Greece he was known as Pan. To the Minoans he was called the Minotaur. He is found in Hindu and Native American mythologies. These horned gods of nature were eventually demonized by the church, and his image was reborn as that of Satan."

"So your parents were devil worshippers?" Joseph asks.

"You're not listening," Rosalyn says. "From a Christian point of view, yes, they were devil worshippers. In the same way that Indians and Africans and Egyptians and Romans were devil worshippers. Gods of the old religions become the demons of the new religions. This is how it has always been. And so the old religions go away for a while. And much information is lost forever. My parents wanted to find all the information they could, because they felt that Cernunnos was more important than anyone may have thought. They were sure this is why so little information about him existed.

"They were surprised to find that depictions of horned gods had been found in cave paintings in France, from the Stone Age. They started doing research in obscure places, and slowly they started to uncover bits and pieces. From the writings of Cicero and Pomponius Mela, and art from Malasia and South America, they were finding similarities between ancient pagan practices and the various gods from around the world. But little could be found about Cernunnos. They searched for over 10 years, but ended up with little more than they started with. Then came the dreams."

"Dreams?" Joseph asks.

"Yes," Rosalyn continues. "My mother began having dreams about Cernunnos. Sexual dreams. In the dreams Cernunnos told my mother that she would have a child, and that child would have a child which would be the mortal vessel for his magnificent return to earth. My father thought nothing of it at first, but then he started having dreams. Dreams of a child running in his home, and of deer and snakes congregating in his yard. My mother was not in his dreams, but there was much happiness and love.

"When my mother became pregnant, the dreams went away. They didn't know what to do. When I was born, it was bittersweet for my father. My mother died during my birth, and my father abandoned his pagan studies. He returned to teaching, and as far as I know we lived a pretty normal life. But when I turned 6, I began to have dreams of my own. Dreams of men with horns, and snakes and deer following me, and when I told my father this, he became scared. I told him everyday of my dreams, they were all different, but very similar. I told him that a magic creature wanted to come home, and that I had to help him. I was so little, I just thought it was a fairy tale I had created. But my father knew better.

"After a while, he began his research again, and he kept a journal of all of my dreams. It became his bible. He became convinced that an ancient god was sending his Holy Word through me. And when the prophecy came, he became more serious and determined to protect me. We came here, to the South, moving through several states, finding the right area to raise me, away from prying eyes. We settled here in Monterey, when I was 11 years old.

"We're in Monterey?" Joseph asks, a little surprised.

"Of course," Rosalyn responds. "Where did you think you were."

"I had no idea. I thought I was taken away."

"No. We're pretty deep in the woods, but this is still Monterey."

"I still don't understand what this has to do with me," Joseph says.

"You are the key that is necessary to unlocking the door that keeps the Horned God from coming home."

Joseph stares at this beautiful, but clearly disturbed girl.

"I'm not crazy," she says. "And I'm not making this up."

"I don't think you are," Joseph says. "I just think you might be a little confused or something. Maybe your father has you brainwashed."

"My father is not the one in control of what is going on here," Rosalyn says sternly. "He is making sure things go as they should, but I am the one who has the dreams. I am the one who tells him how things should be."

"So tell me what you want with me," Joseph says.

Rosalyn gets up, and moves closer to Joseph. She puts her face close to his, and stares deep into his eyes. "We are to be married, tomorrow night. And we are to consummate our marriage immediately, so that your seed and my egg will become one, and lead to the birth of Cernunnos, our Earthly God.

"Married," Joseph says. "You want me to marry you, and then screw you, so we can make a little baby god?"

"Yes."

"Look, Rosalyn," Joseph says. "I am certainly flattered, but I have to say, and please don't take this wrong, but this is the most fucked up ridiculous thing I have ever heard in my life."

"I'm sure it is, but that doesn't make it untrue."

"But what if you're wrong," Joseph says. "What if it's only dreams? What if there is no Horned God?"

"But there is…"

"But what if you're just crazy?" Joseph shouts.

Rosalyn stares at Joseph in silence for a moment. She seems to be contemplating the possibility that he could be right.

"Then I will owe you a big apology," she finally says. They sit in silence for several minutes. The air around them seems to get colder, the meat hooks seeming to shiver as if they were alive. "I'm sorry that things have to be this way for you," Rosalyn says. "But tomorrow you will see that all you have been through will not have been in vain. Tomorrow, I promise, you will forget about your life before now. You will see how the world is truly meant to be. And you will feel the power that awaits us."

Joseph looks away. Her presence in the room is beginning to disturb him greatly.

"Tomorrow," Rosalyn says, "We will wed, and we will open the door for our God to return to his home."

Rosalyn walks away, towards the door. She stops abruptly, and she turns to look at Joseph. Joseph senses her eyes, and looks up to her.

She has a sad look on her face, like she's feeling pity for him, hanging from the cold chains. Then she smiles at him, and opens the large metal door, slips out into the dark hall, and Joseph is alone again.

He thinks of Allison. He wants to cry, but he's afraid the tears would freeze on his cheeks.

"I love you, Allison," he says. "I love you, and I'm sorry."

ELEVEN

The last several days have left Sheriff Deputy Collin Monroe feeling broken and beaten. He has directed the local search parties, trying to find some trace of Joseph Ethans, and has come up empty handed.

He has fought against local media and other prying eyes, attempting to exploit this tragedy, and he has failed miserably.

Over a hundred local people at some point or another have searched every inch of the fields and a good bit of the surrounding woods in the area where Joseph's truck had been found five days ago.

Now he was done.

The investigation would fall into federal hands, and nothing more would be done. Private citizens could continue searching on their own, and the Ethans family would certainly hire a private investigator.

But it wouldn't matter.

There was nothing in these fields to find. Joseph Ethans had simply vanished from this world.

Driving away from the site where Joseph's truck had finally been hauled away, Collin can not shake the feeling that they could have missed something. Some vital clue that would explain everything. But then again, he'd never been in charge of a situation like this. He wasn't a character from C.S.I. or Homicide or some other unrealistic police drama on television. He was just a hick cop in a podunk town too small to even have a mayor. They were lucky to have their own zip code.

Passing by the large Evangelina Plantation sign, he decides not to go home just yet. He just wants to drive for a while, clear his mind of all these negative thoughts before they get a chance to really break him down.

He turns left, taking his police cruiser onto the long gravel plantation road, driving past the massive grain elevators, and out through the sprawling fields.

Nobody lived out here, so Collin could drive at his leisure without being bothered. Of course, he may run across a stray car or two, probably sheltering teen lovers enjoying a few minutes (or hours) of privacy, but he didn't care. Not today. Let the kids fuck their brains out. At least they'll be going home afterwards.

But there were no stray cars found on the winding road. Instead he finds memories.

As a child, his uncles and cousins would take him this way to hunt. There were several roads out here that lead into the woods, to small hunting camps littered all over this area. He remembers one camp in particular. A large multi-room lodge that was owned by this very old man. The lodge had been treated as a sort of motel, renting rooms to local and out of town hunters.

Hunting is a big deal in Monterey. Always has been. Monterey is well known for the amount of deer in the area. And so it was no surprise that Joseph Ethans had hit a deer and lost control of his truck. It happens from time to time. This was just the first time that somebody had disappeared afterwards.

Before he even realizes it, Collin has turned onto the long road that runs deep into the woods to the big lodge from his memories. He has no idea if the place is even still standing. It was in poor shape when he was a young boy, and he hadn't been out this way in at least twenty years, but he certainly remembered the way.

Two and a half miles into the woods, he sees it. The lodge. And it's in pretty good shape.

"Someone has put some work into this place," he thinks to himself as he drives under a large archway that seems to be made entirely of deer antlers, which hadn't been there when he was a boy.

Pulling up in front of the hunting lodge, he notices a few trucks and a Jeep parked off to the side. If there were people here, he'd have to ask if they'd seen Joseph or anything unusual. But mostly he just wanted to go in to the lodge. If the inside had been fixed up as well as the outside, he certainly wanted to see it.

Collin gets out of his patrol car, and approaches the front door of the lodge. He knocks, and waits patiently for an answer. Sounds of birds chirping and chattering in the woods surrounding the lodge are incredibly soothing.

After a minute, he knocks again, and holds his ear close to the door to listen for any movement inside. There is no sound. The inhabitants could be out hunting. Slightly disappointed, Collin turns to head back to his car.

"Can I help you officer?"

Collin turns back around to see a man standing in the doorway of the lodge. He is slightly overweight, and has a thick moustache.

"Yes, I am Sheriff Deputy Collin Monroe. I've been in charge of a search operation. We've been looking for a young man who went missing last week."

He takes a photograph of Joseph out of his breast pocket and hands it to the man. "Have you seen this man?"

The moustached man looks at the photo. "No sir, I can't say that I have."

"Would it be all right if I came inside for a few minutes?"

The moustached man hesitates for a moment, then politely says yes. He allows Collin inside, and he closes the door behind them.

"I hate to intrude," Collin says, "but the truth of the matter is that I used to come out here when I was a kid, and I just kinda wanted to see the place again."

The moustached man feels slightly relieved. "Oh that is just fine."

"Are you the current owner, Mister --"

"Hennessy," the moustached man says. "My name is James Hennessy. And yes. This was my grandfather's place years ago. I inherited it, and recently decided to come down to fix the place up."

"The lodge looks great," Collin says. "I think I remember your grandfather. He was a friendly old man."

"Yes. I only met him a few times myself, but my mother always spoke fondly of him."

Collin looks around the room. There are animal heads covering the walls, as well as replicas of Native American art. There are many items made of deer antlers. Candlesticks, a hat rack, tables, everything seems to have antlers incorporated into the framework somehow. There is a great deal of snakeskin as well. There is a sweet cooking smell in the air. And a pretty strong smell of jasmine, from the many candles in the room.

"How many people are living here right now?" Collin

asks.

"A few dozen," James Hennessy answers. "Some of it family, some are extended acquaintances and colleagues of mine."

"What sort of work are you into?"

"I am an historian, and a religious scholar. I moved here to Monterey to be around nature, to be away from distractions and continue my studies."

"Sounds like you enjoy your work."

"It is my life," James admits.

James watches Collin walk around freely. Collin is studying family photographs on the wall, testing the floors with the weight of his feet. It almost seems like he is investigating a suspicious location. But he is really just reminiscing about his childhood, about being here with his uncles and cousins. He feels incredibly comfortable here.

"Will you be doing any hunting out here?" Collin asks.

"A little," James says. "I can assure you that all my paperwork is in order."

"I'm sure it is. I'm just curious if you'll be open to letting other people come out to enjoy the lodge."

"Are you hinting at something, Officer Monroe?"

"Deputy Monroe," he says, correcting James. "And yes, if it wouldn't be too much trouble, I'd like to arrange something. I'd like to come out here every so often. I can pay, if that's what you need."

"Of course not," James says. "You are welcome here any time. It would be an honor to have a local policeman like yourself as a guest in my family lodge."

Collin smiles wide, barely holding in his enthusiasm. He doesn't even like hunting really, it's just something about this lodge that makes him want to be here.

"I appreciate your hospitality, Mr. Hennessy. If you happen to come across any sign of that missing boy, you'll let us know."

"Of course," James says.

James Hennessy escorts Collin to the door. They exchange handshakes, and Collin returns to his patrol car outside.

James Hennessy watches from a window as the patrol car backs up, turns around, and heads back out away from the lodge, driving under the antler archway, and disappearing into the woods.

"Does the cop suspect anything?"

James turns around to face the tiny voice behind him.

"No, Rosalyn. He was just visiting."

"Were you serious about letting him hunt here?"

"I am always serious. He seems like a nice enough guy."

"He was familiar to me," Rosalyn says.

"Yes. To me as well," James says. "It was strange. Like I knew him somehow."

"It is almost time, Father."

James looks at his beautiful daughter. He walks up to her, and hugs her tight.

"Tonight will be so very special for you," he tells her.

"Tonight, a new history begins. Tonight, our family will become whole."

They walk together, toward the long hallway that leads to the door which opens to the dark levels of the basement below. James kisses his daughter on the top of her head.

"I only wish your mother could be here. It would have made her so happy."

They go through the door, and disappear into the darkness.

A mile away, Collin is still smiling, driving out of the woods. He can't wait to get home, and make love to his wife, and begin going through his old guns to find just the right one for hunting.

He's not even thinking of Joseph Ethans. He's not thinking of his failures as a deputy. He's only thinking of the lodge, and how exciting it will be to go out there again.

"It was like stepping into Disneyland" he thinks to himself.

"There couldn't be a more peaceful place on Earth."

TWELVE

"It's time to wake up, son."

Joseph opens his eyes. The bright lights inside the cooler are cruel. He's not even sure how he managed to sleep in here.

His hands are still bound high above his head. Still hanging from the chain. His whole body is cold and numb. And now he's looking at the man responsible.

James Hennessy.

World traveler. Historian. Psychopath.

"I'm gonna let you down now," James says. "I don't want you trying nothing stupid."

Joseph does not say a word. He notices that Cliff's body, what they had left of it, is now gone. There is only a tiny comfort in it's absence.

James reaches up and unlocks the clamps that hold Joseph's hands. Joseph begins to fall, but James catches him.

"It's all right, I got you."

James carries Joseph out of the cooler, and into the hallway outside. Joseph is sat down in a chair that had been brought out, and James wraps a blanket around him.

"You'll warm up in a few minutes," James says. "This should help."

James hands Joseph a cup of hot cocoa from a small table nearby. Joseph is cautious and weary, but he takes the cup and sips the hot sweetness.

"I'm sorry for what you've been put through," James says. "We had to follow certain rules. We had to test our guests. Push their limits. We had to know who would be worthy."

Joseph says nothing. The man's words almost sound sincere, if not for the ridiculousness of this whole situation.

These people really believe all this shit? Deer gods? Witchcraft? It's bullshit. Make believe.

"Things will be a lot different after tonight," James says. "We all begin a new journey on a path of ancient enlightenment. And when we reach our sacred destination, we'll have you to thank."

Joseph looks up at the man.

"My daughter came to see you last night."

Joseph nods.

"She told you what our plans are for you, and our purpose for all this."

Joseph swallows some hot cocoa. "It's for your god."

James smiles wide.

"Yes. Our Cernunnos. But you have no need to worry.

This is all a great miracle. I've waited my entire life for this moment. The dreams that my daughter has had, it gave us all the information we needed to prepare for this. But it is all so strange and new to you, I know. I'm sure it has been a little overwhelming."

Joseph looks away.

"This is your day of glory, son."

An unknown man comes around the corner of the hall.

"Boss. I believe we are all ready now."

James nods to the man, who turns and walks back around the corner.

"I wish I could give you more time to warm up, and get cleaned up, but we are all so anxious. It's almost midnight, and it's best if we get this whole thing started."

James takes the cup away, and helps Joseph up onto his feet.

"You're gonna have to walk on your own. Out of

respect for our Lord and our Cause."

Joseph moans a little as his weight pushes down on his weak legs. For a moment he almost falls down, but he remains upright.

"Follow me now, son."

James walks off down the hall, never looking back.

Joseph contemplates running the other way, but he can't. He'd never make it. With great reluctance, he follows James around the corner, and down the rest of the dark hall.

They walk a dozen yards or so until they come to a wooden door.

"There is no turning back now, son," James says. "When we go through this door, you need to open your mind to the ritual and your heart to the power."

Joseph says nothing, he just looks down at the floor.

James reaches up and knocks three times. A rustling

sound is heard on the other side, and then the loud clank of the lock and the door opens.

Inside is a brilliant sight. A wide beautiful room filled with statues of animals and angels, and tall candle holders made of deer antlers. The walls are draped with expensive looking sheets, black and red. On the far wall hangs what appears to be a life-sized crucifix, covered with a large red tarp. The room has the feeling of a church, although there is an unmistakably menacing quality to it.

There are many people crowded into the room. More than Joseph can remember seeing around earlier. There are a few women here too, or so it would seem. Everyone is wearing sleek brownish-green cloaks. Some have the hoods pulled up, obscuring their faces. Some wear the hoods down, and instead wear headpieces with deer antlers attached.

A man brings James a cloak. He slips the cloak on, leaving the hood down.

"Wait here," he says to Joseph.

James walks through the crowd in the direction of the draped crucifix. He steps up onto a large round slab in the center of the floor, which Joseph had not noticed at first.

The slab is made of stone, and is about ten feet in diameter. In the center of the slab is painted a large pentagram, a five-pointed star in a circle.

"My friends," James begins. "My family. I want to thank all of you for being here tonight. It is a tremendous honor to have you all together for this magical night, which we have waited for so many years.

"You all know how hard I have worked to make this event as faithful as possible to legends my wife and I uncovered nearly twenty years ago. My greatest wish is that she could have been here for this, to see you all again, and to celebrate in this miraculous occasion. But she is here in spirit, in the air we breathe, and in the ground upon which we walk, and in the blood that flows within us all. And she lives forever in the heart and soul of our beloved daughter, Rosalyn."

James motions with his hands to his far left. Everyone turns their heads to find Rosalyn, standing proud.

Joseph's jaw almost drops from his head.

Rosalyn is in a majestic white dress, with silk and lace and Celtic knots woven throughout. Her hair has been curled into petite ringlets, and her makeup applied with great care. She is the most beautiful thing Joseph has ever seen in his life.

She is a goddess.

Rosalyn walks up to the slab, and her father leans down to kiss her forehead.

"Tonight we celebrate my daughter's birthday," James says. "She is seventeen years old tonight, and she is about to cross a glorious threshold into a new world, and she brings us all along with her."

The crowd erupts with applause and cheers.

"Now bring the sacrifice, please!" James calls out.

Joseph feels a lump in his throat, then he sees a man with a cage walking towards the slab.

"Set the sacrifice upon the altar," James says.

The man reaches into the cage and pulls out a large rabbit. The rabbit is set down upon the slab. It looks nervous and confused. Joseph emphasizes with it. "In the names of our God and Goddess," James says loudly, "in the spirit of Nature and the cycle of Life, we consecrate this altar with the blood of this sacrifice."

James hands Rosalyn a long bladed knife, and she reaches out and slits the rabbit's throat. The rabbit jumps about, kicking and twitching, it's blood pouring out all over the slab. One can hardly make out the pentagram now.

After a minute, the rabbit quits fighting the inevitable, and it is taken away. James reaches down for his daughter's hand, and helps her up onto the slab. "In the names of our God and Goddess, in the spirit of Nature and the cycle of Life, we consecrate this altar with the flesh of my daughter."

Rosalyn unties a knot on the front of her dress, and the material slips away, unveiling her perfect nude body to the entire room. She shows no shame or embarrassment, but when she meets Joseph's eyes she almost seems to blush just a little.

"In the names of our God and Goddess, in the spirit of Nature and the cycle of Life, we consecrate this altar with the flesh of her lover."

All heads turn now towards Joseph, who had mostly gone ignored until now.

"Come on, son," James says to him. "We don't have much time."

Joseph walks slowly towards the large slab, the bloody altar. He can feel the eyes of the crowd upon him, and he is beginning to feel more scared now than at any other point during his imprisonment here. James reaches down and helps Joseph up onto the altar.

"You have to strip now," James says to him.

Joseph is only wearing pants and boxer shorts, but he is reluctant to take them off in front of so many people. And especially in front of Rosalyn.

"You have to do this," Rosalyn whispers to him.

Joseph closes his eyes, takes a deep breath, and unbuttons his jeans. When his pants and boxers are gone, and he can feel the cool air of the room on his entire body, Joseph opens his eyes. So far, so good.

"Take her hand, son," James says.

Rosalyn reaches for Joseph's hand, and their fingers entwine. "And now, in the names of our God and Goddess, in the spirit of Nature, and the cycle of Life, we consecrate this altar with the presence of our Lord in effigy."

Two men approach the large, draped crucifix and pull away the tarp. The crowd erupts again in loud cheers, and Joseph turns to see the object of their excitement.

Upon the wall hangs a bloody monstrosity. A man, or what appears to be a man stitched together from parts of other men, like a creation of Frankenstein. Arms and hands, even the head, sewn from an unknown number of victims, the seams bloody and rotten.

But it's not only human anatomy that Joseph sees. The entire lower body seems to be taken from an animal, like the legs of a giant reindeer. Antlers are attached morbidly all over the body, like a twisted armor.

And a large set of antlers appear to be sprouting from the abomination's head. All of this, and the thing is tied to a large black cross, decorated with antlers and animal skulls.

"Our Lord, Cernunnos," James exclaims proudly. "He will be reborn, and tonight we consecrate this altar in his name with the marriage of his mother and father!" The crowd cheers madly, and James motions for them to calm down. He looks at Joseph.

"Joseph Ethans, do you willingly take the hand and

heart of Rosalyn, to serve her and the Holy child you shall bring into this world?"

Joseph is shaking. This is all going so fast, he hasn't even had time to let it all sink in. These people are really crazy. Out of their fucking minds. He wants to leave. Right now. But he knows he could never make it out alive.

"I do," he says. James smiles.

"And Rosalyn Hennessy, do you willingly take the hand and heart of Joseph, to serve him and the Holy child you shall bring into this world?"

"I do," she says with no hesitation.

"Then in the names of our God and Goddess, in the spirit of Nature and the cycle of Life, we consecrate this altar with the union of Joseph and Rosalyn, and the consummation of their marriage."

Cheers from the crowd again. James steps down from the altar, and Rosalyn turns to face Joseph.

"This is the fun part," she says as she wraps her arms

around him and kisses him deep.

Her tongue in his mouth is like a drug. He is instantly overwhelmed with a warm calm. Her hands run down his back, brushing against his buttocks. Goose bumps cover his body.

He feels his own hands upon her now, caressing her hips and behind. He can smell her wetness, in that tender spot between her thighs.

He thinks of Allison. Guilt sweeps through his heart.

Rosalyn senses his hesitation, and she turns around, backing herself up against him. She grabs his hands, pulling one to her breast, and the other to her crotch. She can feel his cock swelling behind her, and she grinds back into him.

All thoughts of Allison vanish, as primal lust consumes Joseph. He turns Rosalyn back around, and drops down on his knees. The crowd cheers louder as he works his tongue into her crotch. Rosalyn moans loud, running her hands through Joseph's hair.

The crowd begins to chant, "Cernunnos! Cernunnos!"

Rosalyn joins Joseph on her knees, and she kisses him, grabbing his cock with her gentle hands. She strokes him lightly, then gets down low, taking him into her mouth.

The blood in Joseph's veins feels like fire, and Rosalyn lays down on the bloody altar, beckoning him to her.

Joseph climbs on top of Rosalyn, and he enters her easily. Her body tenses up for a moment, and then relaxes beneath him. Joseph can feel the warm blood around his cock as he thrusts into her.

"Cernunnos!" The crowd chants louder. "Cernunnos!"

Rosalyn forces Joseph over onto his back, and she climbs on top of him. She moves herself fluidly on him, sweat glistening upon her petite breasts.

"Cernunnos," she says softly. "Your time is now. The altar has been consecrated to your wishes."

Joseph finds her talking a little distracting.

"The sacrifice of blood," she says. "The sacrifice of flesh."

She grinds down harder on Joseph. Faster.

"And the sacrifice of lust," she says. "I call out to you, my Lord!"

Joseph is beginning to feel light headed. Something is not right. Then he notices something.

The horned effigy on the wall behind Rosalyn. It's eyes are staring down at them. But that's impossible. He must be imagining it.

"I'm sorry, Joseph," Rosalyn says. "I have not been completely honest with you. I have not been completely honest with anyone."

"I don't understand," Joseph says.

The crowd chants even louder, "Cernunnos! Cernunnos!"

Rosalyn closes her eyes, and her entire body quakes in

orgasm.

"Cernunnos!" She screams, "My Lord, my stag! Your lover awaits you!"

There is a dark movement behind her, and Joseph's blood runs cold when he sees the thing on the wall twitching and groaning.

The chanting of the crowd slows to an uncomfortable quiet, as everyone takes notice of the effigy as it moves upon it's wooden cross.

James Hennessy looks to his daughter.

"Rosalyn," he says. "What is going on?"

Rosalyn just smiles at her father, and she bites her lower lip as the last tingle of orgasm sweeps through her body.

The thing on the wall screams out like a freight train, and breaks free from the crucifix. It collapses to the floor, then unsteadily stands up tall on it's muscular animal legs.

Everyone in the room is speechless, staring at the beast, the thing they had pieced together themselves, according to the wishes of Rosalyn.

Rosalyn.

Everyone turns their heads to look at her.

"And now, my Lord," she says. "I offer you this sacrifice of a hundred heads."

The creature roars loud, like a lion or a dragon, and panic washes over the room.

The creature's movements are awkward but swift. The crowd is screaming, running in all directions as the creature tears through them.

Blood and bones and meat separate from one another, flung about like confetti as the creature makes it's way around the room. The horns that are attached all over it's arms and legs, placed as decoration, are now being used as weapons of carnage and destruction.

Amidst the chaos, the tall antlered candle holders are knocked over, and fire quickly consumes the drapes that cover the walls of the room.

"You can go now," Rosalyn says to Joseph.

Joseph just stares at her. Fear has gripped him, he is in disbelief of what he sees, and his mind can barely keep him from screaming and joining in the frantic madness.

Rosalyn slaps him hard across the face.

"If you want to live," she says. "You have to leave now!"

Joseph gets up and finds his pants. He struggles to get them on, trying not to look at the creature and the massacre it is playing out.

He pushes his way through the crowd to the door, which is still locked. He fumbles with the latch, and it slides away, and the door comes open. He takes one last look behind, and he sees the creature climbing onto the altar toward Rosalyn. It roars down at her, and the crowd seems to be trying to fight back against it.

Joseph turns and runs out of the room, and into the shadows of the hall. He turns the corner and runs past the cooler door. He sees the small chair and table, and his cup of hot cocoa, and he goes around the next corner.

He makes it to the door at the end of the hall, and he enters the small room where Michelle's body was being dismembered, where he put the meat clever into the bearded man's forehead.

He goes through a door on his right, and he is in another room, quite larger. He sees several more doors. This is very familiar to him.

Yes.

One of the doors leads to the cell he was first held in. He closes his eyes to get his bearings. He heads for a door on the far end of the room.

He can hear screaming behind him. Some of the crowd have made their way out of the altar room, and they are coming down the main hall.

Joseph goes through the door, and he finds a set of old wooden stairs. He knows it's the stairs he was dragged up before.

He runs up the stairs. When he reaches the top he can smell food. He follows the smell into the dining room, with the table he and the others had been sat down at.

He runs out of the room, and into a hallway with many doors. Bedrooms, he notices, as he rushes past them. The screaming behind him again. The others have reached the stairs. Joseph runs faster.

He finds himself in the living room now, with beautiful furniture and tables made with antlers. And a very strong smell of jasmine from candles. The smell fills his lungs, and Joseph almost gets sick.

Then he sees the door. It has to be the way out. He opens the door, and runs out into the cool night air. The rocks on the ground hurt his bare feet as he runs down the driveway. He stops at a large archway made of antlers, and looks back at the lodge.

A man comes running out through the front door with a shotgun. Another man comes running out, his cloak on fire.

Joseph runs off into the woods. He runs about a quarter mile or so, and he can hear screams and gunshots in the darkness behind him. The creature is in the woods. It is killing everyone it gets it's hands on. Joseph runs harder.

His muscles hurt, and his broken bones grind into his nerves, but he won't stop. He can't stop. He has to get out of this. He can't allow himself to be a victim of some unbelievable monster.

Allison.

Think of Allison.

And mom and dad. And Malcolm.

Keep running. You can do this, Joseph.

After another mile, the woods thin out, and Joseph finds

himself running out into a field. Ahead in the distance, maybe another mile or two away, he sees the lights of the tall grain elevators.

Evangelina Plantation. He can't believe it.

He has a good idea of where he is now. Make it to the grain elevators, and then he can find the road to the highway.

The screams and gunshots are getting closer now. Joseph sprints out through the field, trying to avoid tripping over the long rows of soil that stretch out for acres.

After about a mile, Joseph turns to look back towards the woods. In the faint moonlight he sees a man with a gun come running out into the field. He is quickly followed by the unmistakable size and speed of the creature.

The man stops to fire his gun at the creature, and Joseph feels the ground disappear below his feet. He tumbles down into a drainage ditch about five feet deep. He tries to get up again, but it's no use. The pain is too much.

He hears a scream far behind in the night, and Joseph closes his eyes, giving in to darkness.

———————

Nearly an hour passes before Joseph wakes up again. The night is quiet and still. No screaming. No gunshots. He can't move at all. It takes most of his energy just to breathe.

"You're awake."

Joseph turns his head slowly and finds Rosalyn kneeling nearby. She is still nude, still beautiful, still like a goddess. Then he sees the creature standing several feet behind her.

Joseph gasps, and tries to back away, but his muscles are too sore.

"It's all right," Rosalyn says. "Cernunnos will not harm you. He wants to thank you."

Joseph strains to speak. "For what?"

"For helping to bring him back," Rosalyn says. "He wants you to know that if he were stronger, he would help you. But I'm afraid it is too soon. He is still too weak."

"He didn't look too weak," Joseph says, thinking of the madness in the altar room.

"Physically he is okay," Rosalyn says. "But his other abilities will take some time."

"Can you take me someplace," Joseph asks. "Leave me somewhere, so I can get help."

"You've lost a lot of blood," Rosalyn says. "And we can not risk being seen. Not yet."

Joseph looks away.

"I'm sorry I lied to you about your purpose in this," she says. "I'm sorry I had to use you. But it was the only way. I was not meant to be my Lord's mother. I am his lover. His bride."

Joseph looks at her again.

"I am going to be his Goddess," she says.

Joseph looks over at the creature, Cernunnos. Shadows obscure his features, but the moonlight gives his eyes an otherworldly quality. Joseph looks away.

"I can help you go quickly," Rosalyn says. "If you want."

"What I want," Joseph says, "is to see Allison again."

Rosalyn's face grows sad, concerned. "I'm sorry, Joseph. But that is not going to happen."

Joseph feels his eyes begin to water. Rosalyn leans over him.

"Let me do this for you. It will not hurt."

Joseph closes his eyes, and nods his head. Rosalyn leans down and kisses him on the forehead, then places her hand over his mouth. With her other hand, she pinches his nose.

Joseph struggles a little, fighting for breath, but he is too tired. Too weak. It only takes a few seconds, and Rosalyn feels Joseph's body go limp, and she lets him go.

She stares down at his body for a few moments, and she begins to cry. Cernunnos reaches out and places his hand on her shoulder, letting a small grunt escape his throat.

Rosalyn stands up, and wipes the tears from her eyes. She takes the hand of her lover, her God, and they run through the darkness towards the woods.

THIRTEEN

When Sheriff Deputy Collin Monroe gets the phone call at 11:00 AM to come out to Evangelina Plantation, he doesn't want to think about it. He knew this entire situation would end in a bad way.

But bad things happen all the time. There's not much one can do about it.

Seeing the line of police vehicles on the side of the road near the plantation grain elevator, he puts on his professional face. He knows he's not going to like what he is about to see, but he knows he has to pretend like he is still in charge.

At least until the big boys show up.

Walking through the field toward the crowd of officers and investigators, Collin is approached by another officer.

"Farmer was out on his tractor," the cop says. "Just killing time I guess, and he spotted the body in the drainage ditch up this way."

Collin steps to the edge of the ditch, and looks down at the pitiful body of Joseph Ethans. "How long has he been here?"

"We're not sure yet."

"Wasn't this area searched?"

"Several times, sir."

Collin gets a sick expression. "Then he hasn't been here very long."

"You think he was dumped?"

Collin looks around at all the people. "I don't know."

He goes down into the ditch to get a closer look at the body. He doesn't want to, but there might be something being overlooked.

"He has a few broken bones," another cop says. "Probably a lot of internal bleeding did him in."

Collin leans down close to the body, then gets an odd expression on his face. "What's this smell?"

"Smell?" The cop asks.

Collin breathes in deep. Then it hits him.

"Jasmine."

———————

Sirens roar and lights blaze as Collin leads a parade of squad cars on the narrow road through the woods.

He sees the archway of antlers, then he smells the

smoke.

Smoke and ash. Burnt wood. Charred antlers protruding from the rubble.

This is all that remains of the hunting lodge.

Collin is already regretting coming here. He gets out of his car, and walks over to where the lodge had stood just yesterday. He is not looking forward to the investigation that will come from this. He knows there is some connection between this burnt lodge and the disappearance and death of Joseph Ethans.

Out of the corner of his eye, Collin sees a man standing in the woods several yards away.

"Hold it right there!" He calls out, raising his gun.

But there is no man. There is only woods.

He lowers his gun.

"Are you okay, sir?" A cop asks.

"Yeah," Collin says. "I thought I saw somebody."

He thinks for a moment, then looks a little confused. "It might have been a deer. I must have spooked it. I'm not sure..."

The other cops look around at each other.

"I think you should get some rest, sir," the cop tells him.

"Yeah..."

Collin walks slowly toward his car. It's been a long week. He does feel pretty tired.

But mostly he feels disappointed. He won't be visiting the hunting lodge like he had hoped. He almost wants to cry.

Keep your professional face on, Collin.

He gets in his car and turns the radio on.

Johnny Cash.

Singing about places he'd been. He's been everywhere, man.

And Collin looks out the window at the smoking remains of the hunting lodge, and he knows.

He's not going anywhere.

EPILOGUE

Miles in the woods surrounding Monterey, Louisiana, a beautiful girl with long red hair sleeps nude on the cool ground. Morning dew shining like glitter on her skin. She had a long night, and she is exhausted.

Nearby sits her lover, her God, who watches her sleep. He has never felt so happy. Never felt so... at home.

A noise catches his attention. He turns his head to see a small fawn standing about twenty feet away.

He smiles at the young deer, which seems to be trying to decide if the stranger is friend or foe.

After a moment, the deer settles down upon the ground to rest, satisfied that it is safe in the company of the stranger.

Cernunnos breathes in the cool morning air, and closes his eyes.

Everything is calm, now. Everything is perfect.

Nothing shall ever be the same.

CHUCK MORGUE is a writer and artist living in Baton Rouge, Louisiana, with his wife and children.

THE HORNS OF EVANGELINA is his first book.